Sports Illustrated KIDS

GOODNIGHT FOOTBALL

BY MICHAEL DAHL ILLUSTRATED BY CHRISTINA FORSHAY

PICTURE WINDOW BOOKS
A CAPSTONE IMPRINT

It's the end of the week,
it's the best of all sights —
beneath the night sky
lies a field of bright lights!

And the bleachers are full, for a very good reason.

The big game is tonight! It’s football season!

The big band plays, and the cheerleaders shout!

And everyone
cheers as the
teams run out!

The fans are excited.
It's time for some fun!

Then a whistle — the kickoff!
The game has begun!

On third and one, the ball is snapped.

But the defense
breaks through,
and the
quarterback's
sacked!

He shakes it off and gets up,
the crowd yells, “Hooray!”

Then the team
huddles up
and discusses
a play.

The quarterback drops back and lets the ball go.

It sails through the air.

Oh, what a throw!

A receiver
breaks loose
and stands all
alone . . .

reaches up . . .
grabs the ball . . .

he's in the end zone!

The teams trade possessions,
up and down rolls the score.

Then a long run wins the game —
hear the crowd ROAR!

What a game! What a night!

Goodnight, players. You fought a good fight.

Goodnight
coaches, as
they shake
hands.

Goodnight, cheerleaders.

Goodnight, band.

Goodnight, bleachers.

Goodnight, fans.

Goodnight field and concession stands.

Goodnight, mascot.
We'll come back soon.

Goodnight, goalposts.
Goodnight, moon.

10

Goodnight helmet
and my favorite
teams . . .

Goodnight, football.
Goodnight and sweet dreams.

TO DANNY THOMAS.

Published by
PICTURE WINDOW BOOKS
a Capstone imprint
1710 Roe Crest Drive, North Mankato, Minnesota 56003
www.capstonepub.com

Library of Congress Cataloging-in-Publication data is available on the Library of Congress website.

ISBN: 978-1-62370-106-2 (hardcover)
ISBN: 978-1-4795-5177-4 (library binding)
ISBN: 978-1-4795-5186-6 (paperback)
ISBN: 978-1-4795-55962-6 (ebook)

Designer: Bob Lentz

Printed in the United States of America in
North Mankato, Minnesota.
012016 009444R